11/25/08

grades 3-4

Fact Finders®

Questions and Answers: Countries

The United States

A Question and Answer Book

by Kremena Spengler

Consultant:
Jeff Passe
Department of Reading and Elementary Education
University of North Carolina, Charlotte

Capstone
press®

Mankato, Minnesota

Fact Finders is published by Capstone Press
151 Good Counsel Drive, P.O. Box 669, Mankato, Minnesota 56002.
www.capstonepress.com

Library of Congress Cataloging-in-Publication Data
Spengler, Kremena.
    The United States : a question and answer book / by Kremena Spengler.
    p. cm.—(Fact finders. Questions and answers: Countries)
    Includes bibliographical references and index.
    ISBN–13: 978–0–7368–6774–0 (hardcover)
    ISBN–10: 0–7368–6774–0 (hardcover)
    1. United States—Miscellanea—Juvenile literature. 2. Children's questions and
answers. I. Title. II. Series.
E156.S668 2007
973—dc22   2006028503

Summary: Describes the geography, history, economy, and culture of the United States in a
    question-and-answer format.

Editorial Credits
Silver Editions, editorial, design, photo research and production; Kia Adams, set designer;
    Maps.com, cartographer

Photo Credits
Capstone Press Archives, 29 (bill); Linda Clavel, 4
Corbis/Ariel Skelley, cover (foreground), 17; Bettmann, 18; David Jay Zimmerman, 11;
    Lindsay Hebberd, 21; NewSport/Matt A. Brown, 19; Roy Morsch, 27; Tom Bean, 25
Getty Images Inc./Stone/Neil Selkirk, 15
The Image Works/David R. Frazier, 13
North Wind Picture Archives/North Wind, 7
One Mile Up, Inc., 29 (flag)
Photodisc, 24
Shutterstock/Brian J. Abela, Xavier Marchant, 23; Jonathan Larsen, 1, 9; Michael
    Thompson, cover (background); Stephen Coburn, 8

1 2 3 4 5 6 12 11 10 09 08 07

Table of Contents

Features

Where is the United States?

The United States is in North America, between the Atlantic and Pacific Oceans. Most states are south of Canada and north of Mexico.

Most of the United States has warm summers and cold winters. Cold and snowy winters are more common in the north. Summers tend to be hotter in the south.

The Rocky Mountains form a natural division between the middle of the United States and the west.

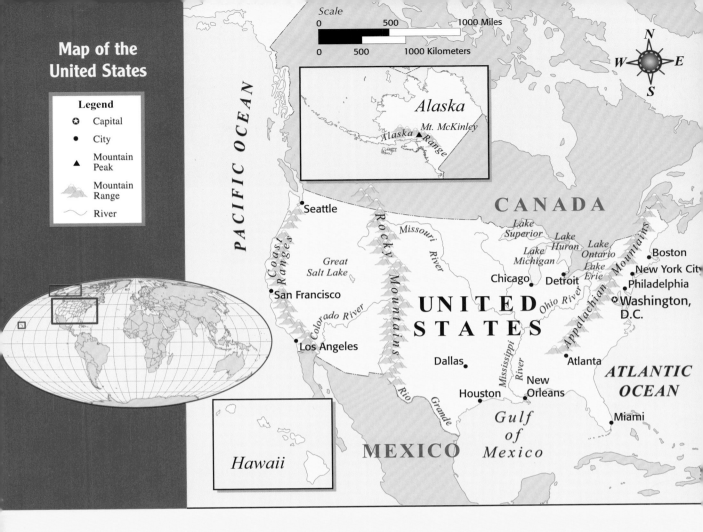

Map of the United States

Legend

- ✪ Capital
- ● City
- ▲ Mountain Peak
- Mountain Range
- ～ River

Scale

0   500   1000 Miles

0   500   1000 Kilometers

PACIFIC OCEAN

Alaska

Mt. McKinley

Alaska Range

CANADA

Seattle

Rocky Mountains

Missouri River

Lake Superior

Lake Huron

Lake Michigan

Lake Ontario

Lake Erie

Appalachian Mountains

Boston

New York Cit

Philadelphia

Washington, D.C.

Chicago

Detroit

Coast Ranges

Great Salt Lake

San Francisco

Colorado River

UNITED STATES

Ohio River

Los Angeles

Dallas

Mississippi River

Atlanta

ATLANTIC OCEAN

Houston

New Orleans

Rio Grande

Gulf of Mexico

Miami

MEXICO

Hawaii

Because of its size, the United States has many different landforms. To the east, the Appalachian Mountains run north to south. The country's middle is a broad plain. The Rocky Mountains, high plains, and deserts make up much of the west.

5

When did the United States become a country?

The United States of America became a country in 1776. In that year, 13 **colonies** declared independence from Great Britain. They fought the British in the Revolutionary War (1776–1783) and won their freedom.

In 1803, the country grew to the west after buying land from France. Settlers rushed in to grab land. This caused many clashes with Native Americans who already lived in those areas. Many were forced off their land.

Fact!

Puerto Rico is a U.S. territory that governs itself, but it's not a state. Puerto Ricans are U.S. citizens, but they cannot vote in U.S. presidential elections. Puerto Ricans voted three times not to change this arrangement.

Colonists fought against red-coated British soldiers at Bunker Hill near Boston. It was one of the first battles in the Revolutionary War.

By the 1840s, many Americans believed their country should stretch to the Pacific Ocean. Through wars and agreements, they added Texas, California, New Mexico, and Oregon. In 1959, Alaska and Hawaii became the last states to join the union.

What is the U.S. form of government?

The United States is a **federal republic** of 50 states. The federal government has three parts, or branches.

The **executive** branch includes the president, vice president, and **cabinet**. The president leads the country. Cabinet members lead departments and give advice on defense, education, and other matters.

The Supreme Court and other courts make up the **judicial** branch. They decide how to apply the laws.

Fact!

The U.S. Constitution, approved in 1787, describes how the government should work. It also protects people's rights.

8

The U.S. Senate and the House of Representatives both meet in the Capitol Building in Washington, D.C.

The **legislative** branch, **Congress**, makes the federal laws. It includes the Senate and House of Representatives. Each state elects two senators. The 435 House seats are divided among states based on population.

What kind of housing does the United States have?

Most American families own houses in cities or **suburbs**. Grass lawns surround these homes. Houses usually have one or two stories. Houses have a kitchen, dining room, living room, several bedrooms, and a bathroom. Most American homes have running water, plumbing, and electricity.

Where do people live in the United States?

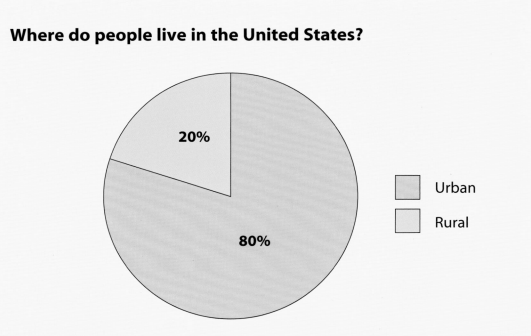

20%

80%

Urban

Rural

Many suburbs have small clusters of homes that form neighborhoods. These developments are often carefully planned.

Some Americans live in apartments. People usually rent apartments for several months or years rather than buy them.

A small number of people live on farms in the country. Farmhouses are similar to city houses, but neighbors' homes can be far away.

What are U.S. forms of transportation?

Road travel is more common in the United States than anywhere else in the world. Many families own two or more cars. Many teenagers drive to school. Large trucks carry goods around the country.

To handle this traffic, the United States has modern highways. **Interstate** highways cross the state borders. These roads have several lanes and no stoplights.

Fact!

Many Americans travel great distances to be with their families and friends over the holidays. During these periods, air travel rises by about 25 percent.

U.S. highways may have many lanes for traffic and ramps that help drivers get on and off the road quickly.

The United States has a large airline industry. All major cities have airports. Travel between cities is common.

Most U.S. railroads carry goods. Passenger travel by train is less common than in other countries. Many cities, however, use railroads or subways for public transit.

What are the United States' major industries?

Farming, manufacturing, and the service industry help make the U.S. **economy** the world's largest. Its land provides many resources used in industries such as oil, chemicals, and steel.

American companies are very advanced in **technology** industries. They produce computers, medical equipment, and cars.

Most Americans hold service jobs. Some work in banks, schools, or hospitals. Others manage businesses or design products.

What does the United States import and export?	
Imports	**Exports**
oil	*technology*
consumer goods	*cars*
cars	*aircraft*

Many Americans follow trading on the stock market. They buy shares in companies in the hopes of sharing in their profits.

Less than one percent of Americans farm. Some of these farms are the world's largest and most productive. Modern equipment helps to grow corn, wheat, and soybeans. Farms also produce meat and dairy products.

What is school like in the United States?

Schools in the United States are public or private. Public schools are free to local residents. Private schools charge fees.

School is required starting with first grade. Elementary school generally goes up to fifth or sixth grade. These students have one teacher for most subjects. Sixth, seventh, and eighth grades are often called middle school. Middle-school students may have a different teacher for each of their classes.

Fact!

Unlike many other countries, American high schools have competitive sports programs. Students join teams and compete against other schools. Some students win scholarships for college based on their sports ability.

Many students in the United States travel by bus or car to their schools.

High school runs from ninth to twelfth grade. Some subjects, such as math, science, and English, are required in high school. Students can choose other courses, such as music and art. High-school graduates may go on to attend a college or technical school.

What are Americans' favorite sports and games?

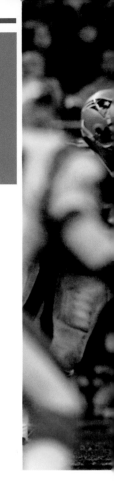

Americans enjoy many kinds of sports, but baseball is known as the national pastime. More people have attended a major league baseball game than games in all other sports combined.

Americans love football. Each year, the Super Bowl is the most watched television event in the country. Fans also keep track of college teams and players.

Fact!

Many people consider Babe Ruth (1895–1948), who played for the Boston Red Sox and the New York Yankees, to be the best baseball player of all time. He set many records.

People all around the world watch the Super Bowl on television. Here, Tom Brady of the New England Patriots throws a pass during the championship game in 2004.

Other sports also have many fans. Basketball, ice hockey, auto racing, golf, soccer, and rodeo are all very popular in the United States.

Americans jog, bike, or ski to stay healthy and have fun. Many people exercise and play sports at fitness centers.

What are traditional U.S. art forms?

American music and movies make a huge impact on the world. Millions of people listen to jazz, rhythm and blues, country, and other music that started in the United States. American film studios produce many of the world's most popular movies.

American writers have created their own cultural tradition. Nathaniel Hawthorne, Herman Melville, Mark Twain, and other writers wrote about American life.

Fact!

American architects built the world's first skyscrapers. The United States has some of the world's tallest and most famous buildings, such as the Empire State Building in New York City and the Sears Tower in Chicago.

People of the Navajo tribe often use bright colors, shapes, and patterns to tell a story in the blankets and rugs they weave.

Most U.S. regions have their own craft traditions. For example, Navajo and Hopi artists in the southwest make beautiful jewelry and rugs. The Appalachian Mountains region is known for its quilts.

What holidays do Americans celebrate?

Many U.S. holidays are related to American history. Independence Day on July 4 celebrates the founding of the United States. People display the flag and watch fireworks and parades.

Thanksgiving celebrates a feast shared by Native Americans and the first colonists, called Pilgrims. Today, families gather for a traditional meal of turkey, cranberry sauce, and pumpkin pie.

What other holidays do people in the United States of America celebrate?

New Year's Day	Labor Day
Martin Luther King, Jr., Day	Columbus Day
Presidents' Day	Halloween
Memorial Day	Veterans Day

Fireworks are a common way that Americans celebrate freedom on the Fourth of July.

Other holidays come from several religions. Christians celebrate Christmas. They decorate trees and give each other gifts. Jewish people celebrate Passover with a special meal called a *seder*. Muslims observe a period of fasting called Ramadan.

What are the traditional foods of the United States?

Most American meals contain beef, pork, or chicken. They are often served with potatoes, peas, green beans, corn, or other side dishes.

Hamburgers, hot dogs, and macaroni and cheese are typical American foods. A hamburger is a ground beef patty inside a bun. It is often served with French fried potatoes. Hot dogs are sausages served inside a roll. Macaroni and cheese is a creamy pasta dish loved by children.

Fact!

Apple pie is a traditional American dessert. It has a pastry crust on the top and bottom, with apple filling in the middle. The popularity of this dish led to the expression "as American as apple pie."

Fast food restaurants became popular because people liked to be served meals quickly.

Many ethnic groups have influenced American cooking. For example, Italian settlers brought pastas, sauces, and olive oil. Germans cooked sausages and cabbage. Chinese cooks served meat or seafood in soy sauce with rice and vegetables.

What is family life like in the United States?

Unlike other countries, American households usually include only parents and children. Most children live with their parents until they go to college or find a job.

In most families, both parents work outside the home. Children help with chores and may receive an allowance.

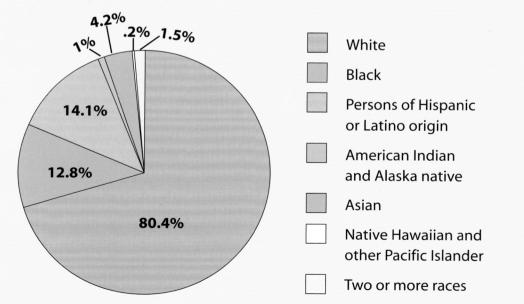

What are the ethnic backgrounds of people in the United States?

4.2%
1%
.2%
1.5%
14.1%
12.8%
80.4%

- White
- Black
- Persons of Hispanic or Latino origin
- American Indian and Alaska native
- Asian
- Native Hawaiian and other Pacific Islander
- Two or more races

Though they may live far apart during the year, family members come together for reunions or other special occasions.

In their spare time, Americans relax with family and friends, watch television, work in their yards, and use computers to shop or play games. Many people visit large shopping centers, or malls. Some people volunteer with their school, church, or local groups.

USA Fast Facts

Official name:

United States of America

Land area:

3,573,438 square miles
(9,161,923 square kilometers)

**Average annual precipitation
(Washington, D.C.):**

40 inches (102 centimeters)

**Average July
temperature
(Washington, D.C.):**

89 degrees Fahrenheit
(32 degrees Celsius)

**Average January
temperature
(Washington, D.C.):**

42 degrees Fahrenheit
(6 degrees Celsius)

Population:

295,734,134

Capital city:

Washington, D.C. (District
of Columbia)

Languages:

English (82 percent), Spanish
(11 percent), others

Natural resources:

coal, copper, lead, uranium,
bauxite, gold, iron, mercury,
nickel, potash, silver, zinc, oil,
natural gas, timber

Religions:

Protestant	52%
Roman Catholic	24%
Mormon	2%
Jewish	1%
Muslim	1%
None/Other	20%

Money and Flag

Money:

The United States' money is the dollar. One dollar equals 100 cents.

Flag:

The U.S. flag has 13 horizontal stripes of red and white. They stand for the 13 original colonies that made up the United States. A blue rectangle in the upper corner has 50 white, five-pointed stars. The stars stand for the 50 states.

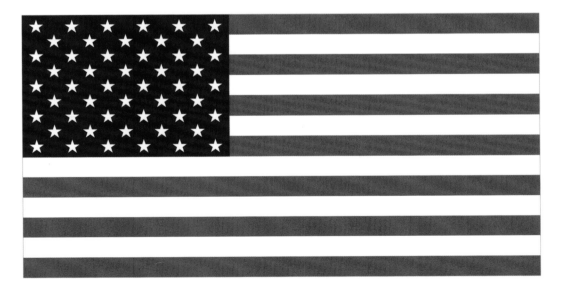

Learn about American English

What do you call a carbonated drink? In some parts of the country it might be called soda. But that's not what everyone in the United States calls it. People in different parts of the country sometimes have different names for the same things. Below are some other words that can vary depending on where you live.

faucet (north).. spigot (south)
pop (midwest) .... soda (northeast)
firefly (north) .... lightning bug (midland)
dragonfly (north/west)... skeeter hawk (south)
bag (north) .... poke (south)
teeter-totter (north and west) .... seesaw (midland)

Glossary

cabinet (KAB-uh-nit)—a group of people who lead government departments

colony (KAW-luh-nee)—a place that is settled by people from another country and is controlled by that country

Congress (KAWN-gres)—the branch of government that makes laws in the United States

economy (ee-KAW-nuh-mee)—the ways in which a country handles its money and resources

executive (eg-ZEK-yoo-tiv)—to do with the branch of government that makes sure the laws are obeyed

federal republic (FEH-duh-ruhl ree-PUHB-lik)—a form of government with elected leaders at both local and national levels

interstate (IN-tuhr-stayt)—going between two or more states

judicial (joo-DISH-uhl)—to do with the branch of government that explains and interprets the laws

legislative (leh-juh-SLAY-tuhv)—to do with the branch of government that makes the laws

republic (ree-PUHB-lik)—a form of government in which people elect their leaders

suburb (SUH-buhrb)—a town or village very close to a city

technology (tek-NOL-uh-jee)—the use of science to do practical things, such as designing complex machines

Internet Sites

FactHound offers a safe, fun way to find Internet sites related to this book. All of the sites on FactHound have been researched by our staff.

Here's how:
1. Visit *www.facthound.com*
2. Choose your grade level.
3. Type in this book ID **0736867740** for age-appropriate sites. You may also browse subjects by clicking on letters, or by clicking on pictures and words.
4. Click on the **Fetch It** button.

FactHound will fetch the best sites for you!

Read More

Doak, Robin S. *United States of America.* First Reports. Minneapolis, Minn.: Compass Point Books, 2004.

Hess, Debra. *The American Flag.* Symbols of America. New York: Benchmark Books, 2004.

Marquette, Scott. *Revolutionary War.* America at War. Vero Beach, Fla.: Rourke, 2003.

Index